Stay

A Girl, a Dog, a Bucket List

For people who love dogs,
and for dogs who love people

A FEIWEL AND FRIENDS BOOK
An imprint of Macmillan Publishing Group, LLC

STAY: A GIRL, A DOG, A BUCKET LIST. Text copyright © 2017 by Kate Klise.
Illustrations copyright © 2017 by M. Sarah Klise. All rights reserved.
Printed the United States of America by Phoenix Color, Hagerstown, Maryland
For information, address Feiwel and Friends, 175 Fifth Avenue, New York, NY 10010.

Our books may be purchased in bulk for promotional, educational, or business use.
Please contact your local bookseller or the Macmillan Corporate and Premium Sales Department
at (800) 221-7945 ext. 5442 or by e-mail at MacmillanSpecialMarkets@macmillan.com.

Library of Congress Cataloging-in-Publication Data
Names: Klise, Kate, author. | Klise, M. Sarah, illustrator.
Title: Stay : a girl, a dog, a bucket list / written by Kate Klise ;
illustrated by M. Sarah Klise.
Description: First edition. | New York : Feiwel & Friends, [2017] |
Summary: Eli the dog has been with Astrid since she was a baby, and now that
Eli is getting older and slowing down, Astrid wants to make fun memories with him,
but knows what is most important to Eli is the time he spends with Astrid.
Identifiers: LCCN 2016037930 | ISBN 978-1-250-10714-5 (hardback)
Subjects: | CYAC: Human-animal relationships—Fiction. | Dogs—Fiction. |
Old age—Fiction. | Pets—Fiction. | BISAC: JUVENILE FICTION / Animals / Dogs. |
JUVENILE FICTION / Social Issues / Death & Dying.
Classification: LCC PZ7.K684 Stk 2017 | DDC [E]—dc23
LC record available at https://lccn.loc.gov/2016037930

Book design by M. Sarah Klise and Eileen Savage

Feiwel and Friends logo designed by Filomena Tuosto

First Edition—2017

The art was created with acrylic paint on bristol board.

3 5 7 9 10 8 6 4 2

mackids.com

Stay

A Girl, a Dog, a Bucket List

by Kate Klise   illustrated by M. Sarah Klise

Feiwel and Friends
New York

When Astrid came home from
the hospital, Eli was there waiting.
He was Astrid's first friend.

In time, Eli also became
Astrid's personal bodyguard,

her favorite pillow,

and sometimes her
best hiding place.

Astrid and Eli had many things in common. They lived in the same house,

ate at the same table,

and slept in the same bed.

There was only one difference:
Astrid was a girl, and Eli was a boy.

And a dog.

As they grew older, Astrid began to notice other differences. "I'm getting bigger than you," she said.

Yes, thought Eli, *but I'm getting older than you.*

It was true. For every birthday Astrid
celebrated, Eli had the equivalent of six
or seven birthdays. Sometimes eight.

When Astrid was six, she was still a young girl, but Eli was an old dog. By then, Astrid noticed it, too.

"You walk so slowly now," Astrid told Eli one day at the beginning of summer.

small
50¢
large
$2.00

Popcorn

They stopped in the park to buy
a bucket of popcorn.

"Popcorn is nice," said Astrid,
"but let's pretend we're eating
spaghetti with meatballs."

Spaghetti with meatballs? thought Eli.
That sounds delicious.

After they finished their snack,
Astrid took Eli to the playground.

"Eli," Astrid said, "have you ever been down a slide? You really should before you get too old."

So with Astrid's help, Eli slid down the sun-warmed slide.

That was fun, Eli thought. *Who knew?*

"I'm going to make a list," Astrid said, "of all
the things you should do before you get too old.
We can do everything on the list together."
The first thing on the bucket list was a bike ride.

"I'm not sure I can teach you how to ride a bike,"
Astrid told Eli the next day. "But I can give you a
ride on mine."

And she did.

This is better than riding in a car, Eli thought.

The next day, Astrid took Eli to the library, where they checked out lots of books about dogs.

"I don't know why I've never read to you before," said Astrid. "I'm glad I put this on your bucket list."

Me, too, thought Eli, who enjoyed looking at the pictures.

A week later, they went to see a movie.
Astrid asked for special permission from the
theater owner.

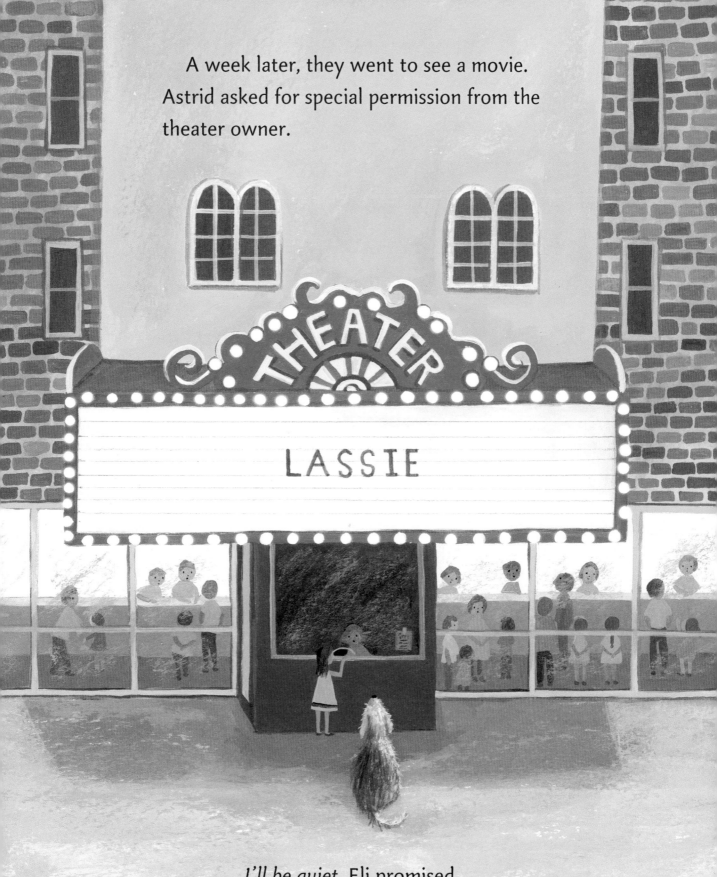

I'll be quiet, Eli promised.

They came home and slept under the stars—
until it started raining.

Then they went inside. Eli slept with Astrid under the covers. That was also on the bucket list.

The following week, Astrid gave Eli a bubble bath. After that, she brushed his clean fur for a full hour. "Look how handsome you are!" Astrid said.

I am handsome, Eli thought.
I'm also very old.

It was true. Astrid knew it, too. So she added one
more thing to the bucket list. The last treat would be
a surprise for Eli.

On Saturday night, Astrid took Eli
to a restaurant for dinner.
"Two plates of spaghetti with
meatballs," Astrid told the waiter.

When their meals arrived, Astrid beamed. "This is what you deserve for being the best friend in the world!"

It is delicious, thought Eli, but I wish we were having popcorn in the park.

As the weeks passed, Eli's fur faded from gray to white. His eyesight became weak. His legs often ached. He no longer had the strength to walk to the park.

So they stayed home and
remembered their happy
times together.

"Is there anything else you want to do before
you get too old?" Astrid asked. "Anything at all?
Whatever it is, I'll add it to the bucket list."

This, thought Eli. *Just this.*

Being with Astrid was the only thing
left on Eli's bucket list.
It was the only thing that had ever
been on Eli's bucket list.